S0-AYY-110

Health & Nutrition

Health & Hygiene

Health & Nutrition

Fitness
Food & Nutrition
Food Safety
Health & Hygiene
Healthy Diet
Malnutrition

Health & Nutrition

Health & Hygiene

MASON CREST

PHILADELPHIA
MIAMI

Mason Crest
450 Parkway Drive, Suite D
Broomall, Pennsylvania 19008
(866) MCP-BOOK (toll-free)
www.masoncrest.com

Copyright © 2020 by Mason Crest, an imprint of National Highlights, Inc. All rights reserved. No part of this publication may be reproduced or transmitted in any form or by any means, electronic or mechanical, including photocopying, recording, taping, or any information storage and retrieval system, without permission from the publisher.

First printing
9 8 7 6 5 4 3 2 1

ISBN (hardback) 978-1-4222-4221-6
ISBN (series) 978-1-4222-4217-9
ISBN (ebook) 978-1-4222-7592-4

Cataloging-in-Publication Data on file with the Library of Congress

NATIONAL
HIGHLIGHTS

Developed and Produced by National Highlights, Inc.
Interior and Cover Design: Jana Rade
Copy Editor: Adirondack Editing
Production: Michelle Luke

QR CODES AND LINKS TO THIRD-PARTY CONTENT
You may gain access to certain third-party content ("Third-Party Sites") by scanning and using the QR Codes that appear in this publication (the "QR Codes"). We do not operate or control in any respect any information, products, or services on such Third-Party Sites linked to us via the QR Codes included in this publication, and we assume no responsibility for any materials you may access using the QR Codes. Your use of the QR Codes may be subject to terms, limitations, or restrictions set forth in the applicable terms of use or otherwise established by the owners of the Third-Party Sites. Our linking to such Third-Party Sites via the QR Codes does not imply an endorsement or sponsorship of such Third-Party Sites or the information, products, or services offered on or through the Third-Party Sites, nor does it imply an endorsement or sponsorship of this publication by the owners of such Third-Party Sites.

CONTENTS

KEY ICONS TO LOOK FOR

WORDS TO UNDERSTAND: These words with their easy-to-understand definitions will increase the reader's understanding of the text while building vocabulary skills.

SIDEBARS: This boxed material within the main text allows readers to build knowledge, gain insights, explore possibilities, and broaden their perspectives by weaving together additional information to provide realistic and holistic perspectives.

EDUCATIONAL VIDEOS: Readers can view videos by scanning our QR codes, providing them with additional educational content to supplement the text. Examples include news coverage, moments in history, speeches, iconic sports moments, and much more!

TEXT-DEPENDENT QUESTIONS: These questions send the reader back to the text for more careful attention to the evidence presented there.

RESEARCH PROJECTS: Readers are pointed toward areas of further inquiry connected to each chapter. Suggestions are provided for projects that encourage deeper research and analysis.

SERIES GLOSSARY OF KEY TERMS: This back-of-the-book glossary contains terminology used throughout this series. Words found here increase the reader's ability to read and comprehend higher-level books and articles in this field.

HISTORY OF HYGIENE

Hygiene refers to the set of practices and habits we follow to help preserve *our health and healthy living. In the medical world and in everyday life, hygiene practices are used to limit the impact of diseases as well as to keep bacteria and viruses at bay. Besides* enhancing *personal health, good hygiene uplifts your mental health by making you feel positive about yourself.*

 WORDS TO UNDERSTAND

ENHANCING: improving

PRACTITIONERS: people involved in a profession; used especially in health care

PRESERVE: maintain or protect

6

MODERN-DAY HYGIENE

In present times, there are specific hygiene practices for different situations, cultures, and genders. We believe in keeping ourselves and our surroundings clean. We are also brand-conscious in terms of which shampoo, soaps, or perfumes to use. In fact, there are thousands of soaps, razors, and perfumes available for us to choose from. There is an endless list of cleaning products, all aimed at providing us with better hygiene options. It is important to know that hygiene is a very old concept related to medicine, personal, and professional care. The old concept of hygiene must be studied if we want to know how modern hygiene practices came about.

EVOLUTION OF HYGIENE

Historically, religion and social practices have played an important role in determining the concept of hygiene. Though it took centuries for hygiene to gain wide acceptance, governments and reformers were eventually convinced of its health benefits. It is interesting to note that far from being uniquely human, the need for hygiene arose almost as soon as animal life did. However, it is also true that medical knowledge was not well developed in the past and thus even minor diseases sometimes proved fatal to human beings. Thus, healthcare practitioners encouraged good hygiene for better maintenance of health.

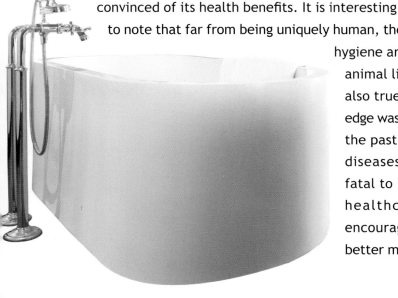
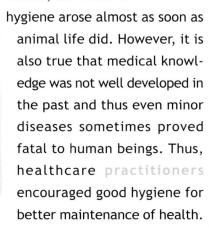

7

EARLY HANDWASHING PRACTICES

Today, washing our hands is a normal, routine activity. However, there was a time when handwashing was optional even for surgeons. In today's world, handwashing is highly recommended for people of all ages, but in the past many children died because of infections caused by dirty hands. Prior to the discovery of soaps, people used only water and the oils from flowers for washing hands. In the early nineteenth century, people started using wash basins for washing the face and hands.

BATHING HABITS IN THE PAST

There was a time when daily bathing was not even considered. Only kings and lords and their households bathed daily. Some had special rooms set aside for bathing, while others bathed in huge tubs brought into their rooms. Among other things, bathing was considered necessary only for women—and not even daily. Gradually, people started using heated water, sometimes mixing it with perfumes, scented oils, and flower petals.

DID YOU KNOW?

- In the early nineteenth century, only the hands, feet, and face were regularly washed, while the rest of the body was washed every few weeks or longer.

8

FOOD HYGIENE

Food hygiene refers to safety and quality precautions taken to keep food safe and healthy. Food hygiene is not limited to the food cooked in our kitchens but also includes the food we buy from the market. Hence, food factories must observe certain housekeeping and hygiene standards, as any negligence in this can adversely affect the health of the consumers. Minor precautions while cooking or buying food can help us avoid infections caused by unhygienic surroundings. It is not only healthy eating, but also hygienic eating that's important for a healthy life.

 WORDS TO UNDERSTAND

ADVERSELY: negatively

CROSS-CONTAMINATION: the passing of bacteria or other contaminants from one thing to another

PARAMETERS: frameworks

9

Check out this video for an introduction to food hygiene.

HANDLING FOOD

While handling food at home, one should take some precautions. Wash vegetables and fruits thoroughly before using them. Avoid using your fingers to handle food. Keep your hair away from food. Use appropriate cutting boards for vegetables. It is difficult to clean some boards, which can result in unhygienic food. We should not cross-contaminate foods—for example, raw meats, poultry, or eggs should not be placed together.

COOKING AND STORING

While cooking food, we should make sure that the cooking area is at some height from the floor. We should not store food for too long in the refrigerator or freezer. Keep the cooking, washing, and utility areas and the aprons and towels clean. It is important to protect the kitchen and food from insects, pests, and other animals. When in doubt, discard food that looks even slightly rotten.

EATING OUTSIDE THE HOME

While dining in restaurants or buying food prepared by others, we should take some hygiene precautions. All cooks, restaurant staff, and those who prepare and handle foods should practice appropriate handwashing. Safe food handling by staff should be enforced in cases of buffets.

BUYING HYGIENIC FOOD

Make sure that you buy fresh meat and fish. Packed food should not be used beyond its expiration date. Raw, cooked, and ready-to-eat foods should be separated while shipping and storing foods.

HYGIENE IN FOOD INDUSTRY

High standards of hygiene apply to food industries as well. Some governments have imposed very strict quality parameters for food ingredients and their storage practices. Laws and regulations have also been put in place to ensure food safety. Consumers have become aware of food safety standards worldwide.

PREVENTION IS BETTER THAN CURE

Prevention is always better than cure—in other words, rather than having to solve a problem, it's better to avoid having the problem in the first place. Hygiene is a key way to prevent problems with food. In our personal kitchens, good hygiene standards are a must, especially for kids, as they are very vulnerable to allergies and infections.

DID YOU KNOW?

- In the 1840s, you would have been more likely to die of contaminated food than from natural causes.

WATER HYGIENE

Because of poor access to safe water and sanitation services, thousands of children fall sick and die every day, and this leads to poverty and reduced opportunities for thousands more. We all know the benefits of clean and safe water. All of us can avoid many common health problems if we observe good water hygiene.

 ## WORDS TO UNDERSTAND

FERTILIZER: a chemical or natural substance added to soil

PRESERVE: maintain something in its original or existing state

SANITATION SERVICES: systems that improve public cleanliness, such as garbage removal and sewage treatment

A THREAT TO LIFE

According to some reports, unsafe water kills more people than any other health problem. Unclean drinking water leads to the spread of diseases such as cholera, typhoid, and childhood diarrhea, which is one of the leading causes of death among children. The effects of drinking contaminated water can be immediate or remain hidden for many years. We must remember that the effects of drinking contaminated water can range from severe illness to death.

CHALLENGES

In many rural areas of developing countries, girls are denied their right to education, in part because schools lack private sanitation facilities. Women spend large parts of their day fetching clean water. Without proper sanitation and water hygiene, social development of a country is not possible.

AWARENESS IS THE KEY

Nowadays, people are increasingly concerned about the safety of drinking water. The development of analytical methods to detect impurities in water has increased awareness among people about clean water. Governments and various global and local organizations are taking steps to ensure that water is tested and regulations are in place so that our water remains free of contamination. Clean water is essential for good health.

13

IMPORTANT PRECAUTIONS

Our own houses and activities are major contributors to water contamination. During rainfall, fertilizer from lawns, oil from cars, and paint residues from walls are often washed into the nearby freshwater bodies, and the same water is used for drinking. Water is arguably the most important ingredient of our food intake, and we cannot live without it. Therefore, one must be certain that the water used, particularly for drinking, is clean. Do not preserve water for too many days; instead, only drink fresh water, and use preserved water for other purposes like bathing.

WAYS TO REDUCE WATER POLLUTION

There are many ways you can help reduce pollution in water. For example, clean the containers in which you store water. Filter water through a clean cloth, and the clear water should be further purified. Boiling of water is the most recommended purification technique since it kills all germs and bacteria. We can also use purification tablets, which are made from chlorine or iodine, to clean water.

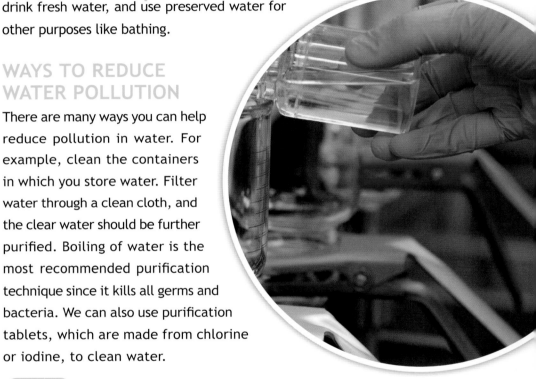

DID YOU KNOW?

- According to WHO (World Health Organization)/UNICEF (United Nations International Children's Emergency Fund), 37 percent of the developing world's population—2.5 billion people—lack improved sanitation facilities, and over 780 million people still use unsafe drinking water.

14

SCHOOL HYGIENE

One of the best places to learn about hygiene is in school. School hygiene education comprises our first lesson in observing hygiene in our daily lives. It is a part of the wider school health education and related to the preservation and development of the health of school children.

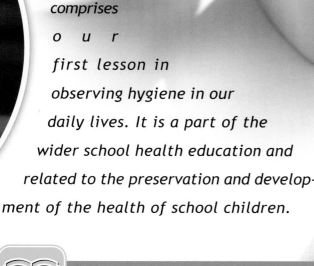

WORDS TO UNDERSTAND

DOMESTIC: relating to the home

MONITORING: observing and checking the progress or quality of something over time

VENTILATION: providing fresh air to a room or building

15

AIMS OF HYGIENE EDUCATION

The primary aim of school hygiene education is to introduce children to useful practices related to personal, water, food, domestic, and public hygiene. It also aims at protecting the water and food supplies of the school and maintaining the cleanliness of the general environment. At the very least, all schools should make provisions for providing basic facilities such as safe water, clean surroundings, quick disposal of waste, emergency lighting, good ventilation, and so on.

THE GOVERNMENT'S ROLE

Some schools have no choice but to manage with poor facilities. Even in schools where sanitation facilities are average, adequate availability of water and a lack of consideration for student needs based on their age and gender can make the sanitation facilities inappropriate for use. Governments must take the initiative in this, ensuring that schools have adequate funding for basic facilities. Not only that, ground-level monitoring of actual use of funds is also needed.

ENVIRONMENT AND LOCATION

Experts say that schools in urban and suburban areas should be located more than 328 feet (100 meters) away from heavy traffic due to the health risks posed by noise pollution from vehicles and the risk of accidents. It may not be practical or possible to observe every recommendation. However, certain things are easier to manage; for example, the school building can be designed in such a way that there is maximum usage of natural light.

POSITIVE DEVELOPMENTS

We all need to recognize that schools have an important role to play in determining the health of a community. Lack of hygiene in schools can cause many diseases and harm to society. If there are no proper school sanitation and hygiene facilities, schools will become places where diseases are likely to be transmitted. The responsibility to avoid that lies on us. A recent survey showed that there is considerable emphasis in schools on modifying the existing sanitation facilities and attending to specific sanitation needs. Schools, especially in urban areas, are considering specific situations related to hygiene, cleanliness, and sanitation, and are making provisions to deal with all of them. It is now understood that investments in school sanitation and hygiene education can help in improving learning environments for students.

DID YOU KNOW?

- As many as half of all pupils regularly avoid going to the toilet while at school and wait until they get home.

17

OCCUPATIONAL HYGIENE

Hygiene at the workplace is as important as it is in the home. After all, the workplace is where adults spend most of their time. The practices developed to prevent illness caused by the working environment are called occupational hygiene. It helps employers and employees understand the risks posed by the absence of hygiene in the workplace and improve working conditions accordingly. It is the collective responsibility of employer and employees to ensure hygienic surroundings in the workplace.

 WORDS TO UNDERSTAND

COLLECTIVE: a group

COMPLIANCE: following rules

IRREVERSIBLE: not able to be undone or altered

REMEDIAL: describes something that is a cure or remedy for a problem

STATUTORY: required, permitted, or enacted by statute or law

18

Check out this video to find out about jobs in occupational hygiene.

BENEFITS OF OCCUPATIONAL HYGIENE

A healthy and happy employee is always an asset to an organization. Hygienic surroundings not only improve the productivity of employees but also help employers in identifying and meeting all statutory obligations and complying with occupational health and safety regulations. In recent years, good occupational hygiene practices have eliminated some historical risks and reduced others. However, hygiene standards are still poor in many parts of the world.

RISKS OF ACCIDENTS

Rather than viewing it as a burden on the organization, it is important to understand the benefits of occupational hygiene. Work is essential for the development and personal fulfillment of individuals, hence the need for occupational hygiene to maintain their health while at work. Many illnesses or disabilities are caused at work. Sometimes the effects of illness are irreversible and can even shorten life. There are too many cases of people losing their lives due to accidents caused at the workplace.

INDUSTRIALIZATION

Rapid industrialization creates chemical and other hazards, such as noise, heat, cold, and radiation. The provision of basic facilities such as clean drinking water and sanitation is not enough to maintain occupational hygiene; the goals of occupational hygiene include the protection and promotion of workers' health, the work environment, and safe and sustainable development.

ENSURING OCCUPATIONAL HYGIENE

One can ensure occupational hygiene at work in various ways. A focus on monitoring health hazards, compliance testing, and remedial action are necessary. Occupational hygiene has evolved with the changing perception of society about the nature and extent of hazards in the workplace, but much more remains to be done. Thousands of workers are affected every day because of unhygienic working conditions, and governments must take firm steps to control this.

OCCUPATIONAL HYGIENE TEAM

The occupational hygiene team can apply several methods to assess the work environment. A traditional method used is a walk-through survey in the workplace to determine the types and possible exposures from noise, chemicals, and radiation. The team can also use advanced technologies like survey equipment or dust sampling. The use of technology depends on the kind of industry being assessed.

DID YOU KNOW?

- According to WHO, occupational health risk is the tenth leading cause of death.

20

ENVIRONMENTAL HYGIENE

Environmental hygiene (also called environmental sanitation) refers to the collective activities of a society to improve the well-being of its people. These activities include providing clean and safe air and water supplies, efficient and safe disposal of animal, human, and industrial waste, protection of food from damage, and adequate housing in clean and safe surroundings. Environmental sanitation is not a stand-alone process but is a set of actions, which collectively aim at improving the quality of the environment and reducing the probability of disease. It includes the management of water, waste, pollution, noise, and more.

WORDS TO UNDERSTAND

COLLECTIVE: relating to an entire group or community
RECYCLE: convert waste into reusable material
STAND-ALONE: capable of operating independently

21

WATER AND WASTE MANAGEMENT

An unhygienic water supply can increase pollution and spread diseases. We should ensure water is treated before being consumed because various chemicals and bacteria can be present in water.

Waste management is the process of disposing garbage. Every day, people throw a large amount of garbage out in the open, which can create environmental hazards.

AIR AND NOISE POLLUTION

Air pollution can affect our ability to breathe, which can give rise to lung and heart problems. Excessive noise in the environment can also cause anxiety attacks or lead to distractions that can cause accidents.

IMPACT OF POOR ENVIRONMENTAL HYGIENE

Poor environmental hygiene—such as lack of sanitation facilities and poor-quality drinking water—cause unnecessary deaths every year. Women and children are the main victims of poor environmental hygiene. After malnutrition, the lack of clean water and proper sanitation is the most important risk factor for diseases globally. Inadequate water, sanitation, and hygiene account for many illnesses and increasing death rates in developing countries.

GOVERNMENT INTERVENTION

There are many cities, states, and countries facing environmental sanitation issues. Some environmental sanitation problems are complex, requiring the full-time attention of engineers. Environmental sanitation issues are receiving increasing attention, but there is still a need for more steps in this regard.

THINGS TO DO

Much can be done to keep the environment clean and help people improve the overall health of their environment. People should reduce water wastage, recycle as much as possible, and where possible, walk or bike instead of driving to reduce air pollution. We should educate other people about ways to improve the environment.

DID YOU KNOW?

- Long-term exposure to loud noises can cause hearing loss.

23

WASTE MANAGEMENT AND SANITATION

In the era of rapid population expansion, there has been an increase in the creation of solid wastes in urban and rural areas. This poses serious hazards to the environment as well as to people. Open-air burning of municipal waste is not a good practice, as it not only increases the carbon dioxide levels but also poses health hazards to trash collectors. Therefore, waste management and sanitation practices are extremely important to keep a check on various health and environmental hazards.

WORDS TO UNDERSTAND

MUNICIPAL: relating to a city

OZONE LAYER: a layer in the Earth's stratosphere

SOLID WASTE: garbage

EFFECTS OF POOR WASTE MANAGEMENT

Poor management of domestic waste can give rise to serious environmental hazards. It leads to the destruction of the ozone layer and may cause life-threatening diseases, such as cancer. It can also affect the drainage system by disrupting the flow of sewerage. Solid wastes also affect soil drainage, which can interfere with the growth of crops, and can be very dangerous to animals and water life as well. Wastes, such as human stool, also cause several diseases. Poor waste management can also be a source of underdevelopment and can harm the tourist industries of affected countries.

WASTE MANAGEMENT TECHNIQUES

In some parts of the world, waste disposal methods are unsystematic and unscientific. Waste is dumped into open areas, which not only leads to air pollution and soil contamination, but also contributes to unhygienic surroundings that are a major cause of diseases. Solid waste should not be dumped near any water body or stream. In residential and office complexes, sweeping should be carried out by sanitation workers daily.

REDUCE, REUSE, AND RECYCLE

Reduce waste generation, reuse it by making some other useful product out of it, or hand it over to the recyclers for recycling. People should be encouraged to reduce the generation of food waste. If possible, they can hand over food waste to animal breeders for feeding animals. All vendors and shops should be asked to request that customers use reusable bags instead of plastic bags. Spreading awareness is the key.

DID YOU KNOW?

- During the eighteenth century, London did not have a sewage system. Toilet water was dumped out of the windows onto the streets, contaminating the city's water supply.

25

MEDICAL HYGIENE

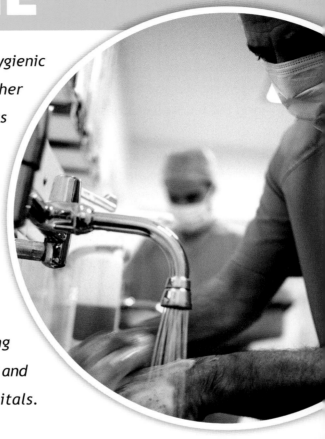

Medical hygiene deals with hygienic practices in hospitals and other healthcare facilities. It works toward minimizing the spread of infections and diseases by cleaning, disinfection, or sterilization. Medical hygiene gives primary importance to the health of the hospital staff, patients, and visitors, and to providing round-the-clock water supply and cleanliness routines in hospitals.

WORDS TO UNDERSTAND

GLUCOSE: a type of sugar that the body turns into energy; often provided to patients in hospitals

PATHOGEN: an organism that causes disease

STERILIZATION: decontamination

STERILIZATION AND DISINFECTION

Sterilization and disinfection practices are used in hospitals and clinics to prevent the spread of pathogens. Disinfection is the process of removing, inactivating, or killing pathogens from a surface. Chemicals that are used in the process of disinfection are called disinfectants. Sterilization is the process in which all disease-causing microorganisms including bacteria, fungi, spores, and viruses present on a surface and contained in a liquid are killed. There are several sterilizing techniques, such as heating, treating with chemicals, and filtering. Sterilization is more effective than disinfection.

HYGIENE PRACTICES IN HOSPITALS

There are plenty of hygiene practices that should be followed by the healthcare staff. Some of them include disposing of infectious objects or materials such as used gloves, syringes, and blood-soaked bandages. Effective treatment of medical waste should be practiced. Rooms of patients, restrooms, and corridors should be cleaned with disinfectant regularly. Hospital staff and visitors should wear masks, caps, gloves, gowns, and goggles to prevent catching infections. Surgical instruments should be sterilized, and wounds and cuts of patients should be properly dressed and bandaged.

MEDICAL WASTE DISPOSAL

Medical waste management is an essential part of medical hygiene and sanitation. If medical waste is not treated effectively, pathogens may enter the environment through air or water, or by direct contact, and

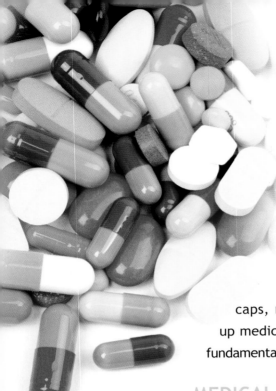

may cause an array of infections and diseases. Sharp medical waste, such as needles and surgical instruments, should be kept separately. Waste should be removed daily, far from the reach of patients and visitors.

MEDICAL WASTE GENERATION

All the waste generated in hospitals and clinics, for example, syringes, needles, medicines, dirty bed linen, used bandages, plasters, glucose bottles, used protective clothing (gloves, gowns, caps, masks), as well as surgical instruments, make up medical waste. The treatment of medical waste is of fundamental importance, as it contains innumerable pathogens.

MEDICAL HYGIENE AT HOME

Medical hygiene at home includes care of the elderly, patients discharged from the hospital, and newborn babies. It is important to give special care to these people, as they are more likely to catch infections. Medical hygiene at home is about keeping sick people and their materials separate to prevent the spread of infections. Sterilizing the items they use, such as utensils, toothbrushes, hair combs, and bed linens is also important. In fact, all normal hygiene practices used at home are also part of medical hygiene, which includes personal hygiene, kitchen hygiene, toilet hygiene, and so on.

DID YOU KNOW?

Methicillin-resistant MRSA (*Staphylococcus aureus*) is an increasingly common disease-causing germ in hospitals. The germ has acquired resistance to drugs and medicines and can cause life-threatening infections.

28

KITCHEN, BATHROOM, AND TOILET

It is very important to keep kitchens, bathrooms, and toilets clean and hygienic. There are some basic rules that one can follow to achieve this. It won't take long to follow these simple rules, and they lead to a healthier environment in your kitchen, bathroom, and toilet.

WORDS TO UNDERSTAND

CUTLERY: knives, forks, and spoons

MOLD: fungus that grows in moist environments

RESIDUE: a tiny amount of something that lingers after the main part is gone

KITCHEN

We need to routinely clean the kitchen to ensure that it is hygienic for preparing food. Following these tips can be of help. Clean the surfaces thoroughly with warm water before you cook and after you've finished. Keep your stove clean by wiping off any spills as soon as possible. Empty the garbage can in the kitchen regularly before it overflows. If possible, recycle all your plastic, glass, and cardboard. Try to wash after every meal. You only need to clean the plate(s) and cutlery you have used to prepare food and eat. Always wash your hands before you start preparing a meal, and afterwards too. Keep cooked leftovers in the fridge and consume them within a few days. Clean out your fridge and freezer with soap and water regularly and throw away any items that look outdated. Throw dishtowels in the wash at least a couple of times a week to prevent the growth of bacteria.

BATHROOM

Bathrooms are in constant use throughout the day. Hence there are a lot of chances for spreading of infection from one family member to another if basic hygiene standards are not observed. Nobody likes to clean a toilet, but it's essential. A dirty toilet can look disgusting, smell

30

bad, and be a ground for dangerous germs.

Always keep a roll of paper towels in the bathroom to quickly clean up any mess. Make sure to wipe down the shower and tub after every use. It may consume some extra water, but it's important to fight the spread of mold. We should keep our drains clean and fresh. We should make sure to clean our toilet tank periodically. Keep the bathroom window closed and use the exhaust fan instead. Don't use soaps that leave a lot of residue behind.

HYGIENE: PART OF LIFE

Hygiene is not an option but a necessity. Good hygiene helps one maintain good health. Therefore, hygienic practices must be taken seriously if one wants to prevent illnesses caused by filth and contamination. No one likes a messy and unhygienic person. Personal hygiene should be a priority for everyone and it should be followed by maintaining hygiene in your home and surroundings.

DID YOU KNOW?

- Most people think of the toilet as the most contaminated part of the house. However, the kitchen sink usually contains 100,000 times more germs than a bathroom or lavatory.

31

PETS

Pets demand serious attention if hygiene at home is to be maintained. We must remember that allergies from pets can cause serious damage to our health and hygiene. People, especially kids, may not even know they are allergic. Always keep your pets hygienic and free from infections. This is not only important for their health but your own health as well.

WORDS TO UNDERSTAND

AIRBORNE: transported by air

FUNGAL: of or caused by a fungus or fungi

LOW-PILE: a type of carpet with short fabric loops

INFECTIONS FROM PETS

Pet owners need to be aware of diseases and infections that can be passed from animals to people. The most common way to get an infection from an animal is by being bitten or by having close contact with them. Some common fungal infections of the skin can be passed on from dogs, cats, and hamsters. Those who work with animals are more prone to these infections.

WARNING SIGNS FOR PET OWNERS

Following are some of the symptoms you shouldn't neglect as a pet owner.

- Smell: When your pets start to smell, it is a clear indicator that they are in desperate need of a bath. Failing to bathe your pets regularly can result in skin problems for them. For dogs, bathing is essential to keep their coat and skin healthy.
- Scratching: Pets with long nails can easily scratch their owners, which can lead to infected wounds.
- Illness and infection: Poor hygiene for any animal can expose it to both illness and infection. Neglecting the hygiene of your pet can prove to be costly for both you and your pet.

PRECAUTIONS

If you want to keep pets at home, you should limit the areas of the home where the pet is allowed, particularly the bedroom and the bed. Limit the use of carpets; they easily attract dust and are difficult to clean. If you must have carpets, choose low-pile carpet and steam-clean them frequently. Wash bedding frequently in hot water. Washing flushes away dust and allergies that have settled on the bedding. Do not allow the pet in the car; if you do allow them in your vehicle, use washable seat covers. Wash your hands after playing with your pet. Bathing the pet every week may reduce airborne allergens. Use a pet allergy brush to clean the pet.

This video offers some great advice about pet hygiene.

ATTENTION

You may not pay any attention to your pet's hygiene until they start to stink, or they scratch you while playing. It is extremely important that you attend to their needs by keeping them well groomed (bathed and clipped). Clean and vacuum your home regularly. Keep surfaces throughout the home clean and uncluttered. Wear a dust mask while cleaning. Forced-air heating and air-conditioning can spread allergens throughout the house. Cover bedroom vents with dense filtering material like cheesecloth.

DID YOU KNOW?

- Bathing your pet weekly can reduce the level of allergens.

34

SMELLING CLEAN

Smelling clean and fresh is an integral part of our personal hygiene. No one wants to be in the company of people who don't smell good. Fragrances, talcum, and good hygiene are important steps toward smelling good. Find the right scents that comple- ment your body and don't overdo the fragrance, other- wise you'll have the opposite effect on people.

WORDS TO UNDERSTAND

ADVISABLE: recommended
CONCENTRATED: undiluted
INTEGRAL: essential

SMELL—PART OF PERSONALITY

How we smell creates an immediate impression about us. Smelling good makes us feel more confident. Even for medical reasons, it is very important to smell clean. If your breath or your sweat smell bad, it is time to see your doctor. There is a strong possibility that you are suffering from some disease. The major challenge with smell is that we don't know that we smell bad until someone tells us. However, it is advisable to not wait until then. Always pay attention to your hygiene and cleanliness.

IMPORTANCE OF SMELLING GOOD

Smelling good is not only important for our health, it is also a part of our personality. Although we do not naturally smell like flowers, there's nothing wrong with wanting to smell pleasant. We all want to smell good to create the right impression. The difficult part about smell is that it takes time to change your natural body smell. Unlike clothes, you can't change it immediately and smell nicer.

HOW TO SMELL GOOD

Smelling good is not something that comes easily to everyone, but is certainly something that requires a good deal of time and proper attention. We need to understand that even wearing fragrances is just part of smelling good, and there's much more to it, such as practicing good oral hygiene as well as bathing regularly. Using a cologne or perfume could be a cover-up in some ways, but practicing great hygiene habits is the key to smelling fresh and clean throughout the day.

USE OF PRODUCTS

There are many products that can be used to smell good. Some of them include:

- Perfumes: There are thousands of perfumes on the market, and they all work differently on different individuals. Avoid using excessive amounts of perfume.
- Essential oils: Like perfumes, essential oils are the concentrated oils prepared from herbs and plants. All essential oils are natural.

DID YOU KNOW?

- Soap and water are the simplest tools for cleaning.

37

SHOES AND FEET

We should work hard to clean our feet and shoes, as they are likely to be affected by unhygienic situations. Sweat can get into our shoes very easily and can facilitate bacterial growth. It is very important to be cautious about the cleanliness of our shoes and feet. We usually ignore them and concentrate on other parts of our body. In summer, we must be very careful with our foot hygiene as heat can make our body sweat in an uncontrollable way and adversely affect our public image.

 WORDS TO UNDERSTAND

ABSORB: soak up

FACILITATE: assist

NUMEROUS: great in number; many

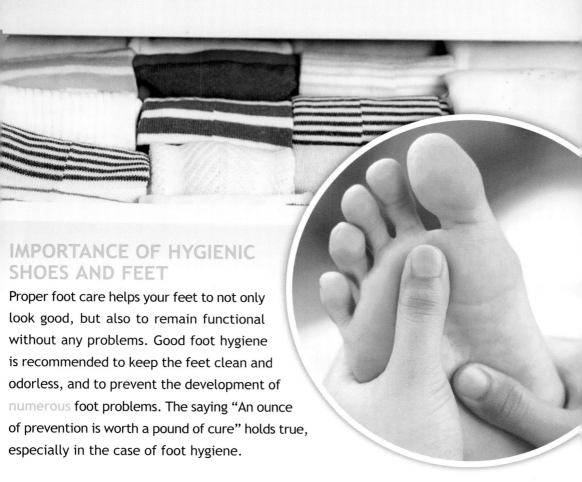

IMPORTANCE OF HYGIENIC SHOES AND FEET

Proper foot care helps your feet to not only look good, but also to remain functional without any problems. Good foot hygiene is recommended to keep the feet clean and odorless, and to prevent the development of numerous foot problems. The saying "An ounce of prevention is worth a pound of cure" holds true, especially in the case of foot hygiene.

EFFECTS OF UNHYGIENIC SHOES AND FEET

Even a small thing like toenails can cause trouble if you ignore them too long. Like every other part of the foot, the toenails need care and maintenance to prevent problems from developing. Keeping the skin and nails healthy prevents the development of infections and keeps the skin smooth and comfortable. One can develop ankle disabilities or other diseases in the absence of regular foot care.

HOW TO TAKE CARE OF SHOES AND FEET

Good feet hygiene is a must for everyone. Some suggestions are given below.

- Choose the right shoes. It is important to think about the comfort of your feet and not just fashion when you buy new shoes. If you have one pair of shoes for school, take them off as soon as you get home so that they can air out overnight. If you have more than one pair, use them on alternate days to allow them more time to dry out.
- Change your socks. If your feet sweat a lot, wash them daily and change your socks often. Try to wear cotton socks, as they absorb sweat well.
- Eat carefully. It is important to learn that food is responsible for a lot of the smells our body carries. Avoid eating onion, garlic, and any other spices.
- Wash properly. It is important to wash your feet daily. If you sweat a lot, take very good care of your hygiene. Also use foot spray for the inside of your shoes.

WHAT'S MORE HYGIENIC: YOUR FEET OR SHOES?

This is an interesting question. We wash our feet at least once a day, whereas we don't ever wash the soles of our shoes! It must be remembered that we can't ignore either of them. Your shoes need as much attention as your feet, if not more. Always try to keep them clean.

DID YOU KNOW?

- The average person walks about 8,000 to 10,000 steps every day.

EYES, EARS, NOSE, AND THROAT

The eyes, ears, nose, and throat are those areas of our body that need more attention in our daily hygiene routine. Allergies, infections, colds, and other problems may prevent the eyes, ears, nose, and throat from performing their functions properly. We can easily avoid them by taking small precautions and care. Learning to look after these parts of the body helps a person enjoy a healthy life.

WORDS TO UNDERSTAND

HOARSE: when the voice sounds rough due to illness or shouting

HYDRATED: with sufficient water

POLLEN: powdery substance released from some plants

41

EYE CARE

Our eyes are sensitive and need proper care. Dirt, dust, and harmful sun rays can damage eyes. To protect your eyes, wear sunglasses when stepping out in the sun. Wear goggles while swimming in public swimming pools. Try to avoid touching your eyes with bare hands and wash your hands often. Make sure to eat a balanced diet rich in iron, Vitamin A, and green leafy vegetables for sharp vision. Maintain a distance of at least a foot while reading a book, watching TV, or working on a computer. When using a computer or tablet for long periods, try to take a moment to look away from time to time to give your eyes a brief rest.

CARE OF THE NOSE

The nose performs the most essential function for humans: breathing. It warms and cleans the air we breathe, which helps keep the lungs healthy. If the air is cold, dry, or impure, the lungs may get damaged. To protect the nose from various infections and diseases, we should clean it regularly. Always use tissues or a handkerchief to blow your nose. Avoid reusing the same tissue or handkerchief, as it might contain germs. Always blow your nose gently, one nostril at a time. Do not put sharp or pointed objects inside the nose, as it might cause infections. If suffering from a cold, use a nasal spray, but avoid overusing it. When possible, avoid sniffing harmful substances such as dirt or pollen, which might cause allergies.

CARE OF EARS

Our ears make us aware of the various sounds around us. Earwax that is produced inside the ear prevents dirt, dust, germs, and small insects from entering. For healthy ears, we should follow some hygienic practices. Clean the ears gently to remove earwax. Always wear earplugs when you're going to be around loud noises. Never put any sharp object inside your ears. Avoid listening to loud music on headphones for long periods. If suffering from partial hearing loss, always wear a hearing aid.

CARE OF THE THROAT

Like the eyes, ears, and nose, the throat is sensitive and also needs proper care. It acts as the gatekeeper and protects the body from disease-causing microorganisms. For a healthy throat, we must follow a few hygiene tips. Avoid shouting or yelling at the top of your voice, as it might damage the vocal cords. Drink lots of water to keep the throat hydrated. Avoid clearing the throat often, as this may cause the voice to become hoarse. Give the throat some rest by keeping quiet for some time. Try to avoid inhaling cigarette smoke, as it can irritate the throat.

DID YOU KNOW?

- Our nose keeps growing throughout our lifetime.

- The human eye is the second most complex organ in the body after the brain.

43

ORAL HYGIENE

Oral hygiene relates to keeping the teeth, gums, and tongue healthy and disease-free. Healthy teeth help us in chewing food and in speaking, brighten the smile, and make us feel more confident. Good oral hygiene means a healthy mouth that smells fresh. It includes clean teeth and healthy pink gums that do not hurt or bleed while brushing.

WORDS TO UNDERSTAND

GUMS: flesh around the teeth

INTERVALS: periods of time

ORAL: relating to the mouth

KEEP TEETH CLEAN

Keeping teeth and gums healthy is one of the most important things we can do for our body. Healthy teeth make a person look good, help in chewing well, and in speaking properly. We should brush our teeth in the morning and before going to bed each night. We should also floss our teeth regularly. Avoid eating too many candies and chocolates. Make sure the toothpaste has fluoride, which makes teeth strong.

PROPER WAY TO BRUSH TEETH

- Hold the toothbrush at a 45° angle against the gums. Now gently move the brush back and forth in short strokes.
- Similarly, brush the outer and inner surfaces of the teeth.
- To clean the chewing surfaces of the teeth, move the brush gently in a sweeping manner.
- To clean the front teeth, move the tip of the brush in an up-and-down manner. Brush for about two to three minutes.

PROPER WAY TO FLOSS TEETH

- Take floss, wrap it around the middle finger of both hands, and hold it firmly between your thumb and forefingers.
- Place the floss carefully between two teeth and pull back and forth gently.
- Now, when the floss reaches the gum, curve it around the edge of the tooth in a "C" shape and slide it in upward and downward motions. Repeat this for every tooth.

45

TONGUE CLEANING

Just like teeth, the tongue should be cleaned at regular intervals. Tongue cleaners are most effective in cleaning the tongue. A tongue cleaner removes small food particles, fungi, dead cells, and the whitish or yellowish coat of bacteria covering the tongue.

TOOTH DECAY

Interactions between the teeth, food, and bacteria lead to the decaying of the outer layer of the tooth called enamel. Bacteria stick to the tooth and form a sticky layer called plaque. When foods containing sugars are eaten, bacteria break down the sugars in the mouth and convert them into acids. The acid attacks the enamel and begins to eat away at it. This causes cavities, which can become painful if they grow large; they can also affect the nerves and gums. Dental cavities are also known as dental caries.

TEETH SENSITIVITY

Teeth sensitivity is very common among people. The symptoms are pain-like sensations in teeth, which are triggered when hot, cold, or sweet and sticky food items are consumed. The pain can occur anytime and can be severe. Teeth become sensitive when the deep layer of teeth, the dentin, is exposed. This may occur because of brushing hard, dental caries, gum diseases, and other dental problems. People with sensitive teeth must use toothpastes especially made for sensitive teeth.

DID YOU KNOW?

The first toothbrush was invented in China in 1498. It was made of carved cattle bone with pig bristles wired into it.

46

NAILS AND HAIR

Good hygiene is not limited to taking care of laundry, sanitation, and food. It also includes thoroughly and regularly washing one's hair and caring for one's nails. These additional grooming habits can reduce the threats bacteria pose to our body. It is important to know, understand, and practice good personal hygiene as early as childhood to ensure a healthy lifestyle even after one moves into adulthood.

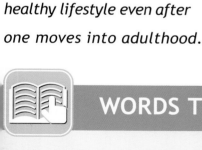

WORDS TO UNDERSTAND

CONDITIONER: a substance that's added to improve the quality of something

MASSAGE: to rub

MINIMIZE: reduce or limit

47

CARE OF NAILS

Fingernails offer a perfect environment for germs to live and breed. Even if we wash our hands properly, there can still be some germs under and around the nails. If they are transferred to the mouth, they can cause serious problems. We should scrub the underside of nails with soap and water every time we wash our hands.

We should cut our nails once a week, ideally after taking a bath. Keep the nails short, as this will help to reduce the number of germs underneath them. Grow nails only if you can keep them clean. Avoid nail-biting, particularly if the nails are being swallowed. Always remember to keep your nail instruments clean to avoid the spread of infection.

HAIR CARE

We have sweat in our scalps, and dead skin cells come off the scalp. The oil, sweat, and dead cells combine and can make hair dirty and greasy. We should brush or comb our hair every time we wash it. Use a wide-toothed comb for wet hair, as it is easier to pull through. If possible, keep your hair short, as this will make it easy to manage. We should brush our hair three to four times a day with a soft-bristled brush or comb.

Wash your hair regularly and rinse it well with clear water. Also, use shampoo, ensuring that it suits your hair type. Massage the scalp well. This will remove dead skin cells, excess oil, and dirt. It is important to note that conditioner is helpful if you have longer hair, as it makes the hair smoother and easier to comb. Avoid overexposure to the sun to minimize the damage caused by its rays.

SPENDING TIME ON HYGIENE

It is very important for us to make some time every day for personal care. Personal care is very important for maintaining good health. Hygiene habits must be picked up from an early age. Even if you have a very busy schedule, daily hygiene should not be ignored.

DID YOU KNOW?

- Hair, especially when long, should be brushed several times a day.

49

SKIN HYGIENE

Skin is the largest organ and is the protective outer covering of the body. It prevents germs from entering the body and causing infections and diseases. It also guards the body's internal organs. Therefore, keeping dirt, dust, dead cells, and germs away from the surface of the skin is of extreme importance. Proper skin care is the key to healthy and hygienic skin.

WORDS TO UNDERSTAND

DICTATES: orders

PROTECTIVE: defensive

UV RAYS: short for ultraviolet rays, a type of radiation

50

SKIN HYGIENE IN HISTORY

In the past, bathing was not considered a good hygiene practice. There have been reports that a monk even asked people to show their love for God by *not* bathing. People across Europe followed the monk's dictates and, in the name of God, refused to bathe. Historians tell us that King John I of England bathed once every three weeks, whereas Queen Elizabeth I took a bath once a month, and Queen Isabella of Spain once boasted that she had only bathed twice in her whole life.

In an attempt to prohibit any type of nudity, early American colonists in Pennsylvania and Virginia declared that bathing was sinful. One law stated that any person who bathed more than once a month should be imprisoned. Untold numbers of people died of several diseases in early times because of poor hygiene habits.

WHY DOES THE SKIN NEED PROTECTION?

Our skin has three layers: the epidermis, the dermis, and subcutaneous tissue. The epidermis is the outermost layer of the skin. It is made up of millions of cells that are constantly dying, flaking off, and being replaced. The dermis lies beneath the epidermis and contains blood vessels, sweat glands, capillaries, lymph nodes, oil glands, and hair follicles. The innermost layer is the subcutaneous tissue, which stores fat and regulates body temperature. If the skin is not cleaned properly, it can encourage germs to cause various skin infections and diseases such as inflammation, rashes, and warts.

51

KEEP THE SKIN HEALTHY

Bathe regularly with an antiseptic soap or shower gel to keep the skin clean. Avoid taking a bath in very warm water, as this makes the skin dry. Make sure to use your own towel and wash it after each use. In addition, never share your towel with others as it may transfer germs. Always pat skin dry and avoid rubbing. Wash your face at least twice a day, especially after staying outdoors. Use a gentle cleanser, face wash, or a mild soap. However, do not wash your face too often, as this may dry out the skin. If too much of the skin's natural oil is washed away, it may become very dry and begin to itch and flake. If the skin's natural processes are interrupted, the skin may begin to produce more oil than usual, which can cause more breakouts.

SKIN AND SUN

The sun emits UV rays, which are invisible to the eyes. These rays can penetrate the skin and cause suntan, sunburns or, in severe cases, skin cancers. Therefore, it is not healthy to stay out in the sun for too long without any protection. Apply sunscreen ten to fifteen minutes before venturing out in the sun. When outdoors, always wear a big hat to cover your face and neck, or carry an umbrella. The heat generated by the sun also makes one sweat a lot which can cause body odor.

DID YOU KNOW?

- The glands present in hair follicles release an oily substance called sebum, which keeps the skin and hair from drying out.

WASHING HANDS

We all know that handwashing is the most important step toward preventing the spread of infection among children and adults alike. We all should wash our hands properly before eating, after using the toilet, or before touching sensitive parts of our body. Washing is essential to avoid bacteria that can cause various health-related issues.

WORDS TO UNDERSTAND

CONJUNCTIVITIS: a bacterial infection of the white part of the eye

INADEQUATE: insufficient or poor

SANITIZERS: products that eliminate bacteria and other microorganisms

Are you sure you're washing your hands correctly? Watch this video to find out!

IMPORTANCE OF WASHING HANDS

Proper and regular handwashing can ensure protection against several infectious diseases. Hand sanitizers can also help keep hands clean. However, one must keep in mind that sanitizers cannot eliminate all kinds of germs. Therefore, sanitizers should not be considered a substitute for handwashing.

EFFECTS OF UNHYGIENIC HANDS

Unhygienic hands can make one vulnerable to infectious diseases that are commonly spread through hand-to-hand contact. Inadequate hand hygiene contributes to food-related illnesses. Eye infections can also be caused by unhygienic hands. It can also increase the likelihood of conjunctivitis or "pink eye." Washing our hands not only helps keep us from getting sick, it also reduces the risk of infecting others.

WHEN TO WASH YOUR HANDS

We touch people, surfaces, and objects throughout the day, and by doing that, we accumulate germs on our hands. Although it's impossible to keep hands germ-free, washing them frequently can help limit the transfer of bacteria.

We should always wash our hands *before* preparing or eating food, treating wounds, taking medicine, and inserting or removing contact lenses. We should also wash our hands *after* preparing food, using the toilet, touching pets, or blowing the nose, coughing, or sneezing into our hands. We should learn to wash our hands after handling garbage or anything that could be contaminated, such as a cleaning cloth or soiled shoes.

HANDWASHING TIPS

The best way to wash your hands is with an antiseptic soap and clean water. Remove any jewelry that you may be wearing. Wet your hands with running water and apply a liquid, bar, or powder soap. Wash your hands with soap and water for at least 20 seconds. Wash the fronts and backs of your hands, as well as the skin between your fingers and under your nails. Rinse your hands well under warm running water, using a rubbing motion. Wipe and dry your hands gently with a clean towel. If your skin is dry, you should use a moisturizing lotion.

Washing hands is an essential part of personal hygiene. It's advisable to develop a habit of cleaning your hands regularly and make this a part of your routine.

DID YOU KNOW?

- According to the UN World Health Organization (WHO), 1.5 million children under the age of five die every year of diarrhea caused by drinking unsafe water, inadequate sanitation, or lack of hygiene.

TRAVEL HYGIENE

It can be challenging to keep up good hygiene when you're on the road, but it's important to do your best, so that you don't succumb to travel-related ailments. It is a good idea to carry a first-aid kit, especially when traveling to areas with limited medical facilities. A traveler should be mindful of his or her safety while traveling to distant lands.

 WORDS TO UNDERSTAND

ENDEMIC: frequently found

PROMPTLY: without delay

SUCCUMB: to yield to an illness

TAP WATER: water that comes out of a faucet

TRAVELER'S HYGIENE TIPS

Maintaining good personal hygiene is one of the best ways to protect yourself from infections and diseases. Check on the quality of the local water supply before drinking tap water or using it for brushing teeth. Wash your hands frequently, especially before or after eating and after using the restroom. Dry your hands with a paper towel before touching anything. Consider wearing a mask when traveling in polluted or crowded areas.

FOOD AND WATER SAFETY

Eating contaminated food is one of the main causes of food poisoning. It is one of the most common travel-related illnesses. To avoid food poisoning, a traveler must avoid eating street food from unhygienic places. Make sure that you eat at clean restaurants and carry some healthy snacks with you. Try to drink lots of water while traveling, but make sure the water is not contaminated. Eat well-cooked food that is served steaming hot. Canned foods, fruits, vegetables, and nuts with thick skins are also good choices during travel. Never wash food items with tap water; use bottled water instead. Avoid eating undercooked fish, milk, and seafood.

TRAVEL FIRST-AID KIT

Carry a first-aid kit while traveling anywhere. Some of the most common items that should be included in the kit are a thermometer, scissors, bandages, antibiotic cream, aspirin, antiseptic powder or solution, and medicines prescribed by a doctor.

57

TRAVEL-RELATED DISEASES

Most travel-related diseases can be prevented and treated easily. According to the World Health Organization, the major causes of illness while traveling include:

- Traveler's diarrhea is one of the common diseases affecting travelers around the world. To reduce the risks of traveler's diarrhea, consume bottled water and hygienic food. Taking antibiotics usually helps, but the disease can turn severe if not treated promptly.

- Malaria is a parasitic disease, common in tropical and subtropical countries where mosquitoes breed abundantly. Poor sanitation is one of the main causes of mosquito breeding. Use mosquito repellants to avoid contact with mosquitoes or avoid traveling to places where malaria is an epidemic.

- Hepatitis is one of the most common travel diseases. It is caused by consuming contaminated food or water. The disease can spread from one person to another, especially if poor personal hygiene is a factor. Travelers should get vaccinated before traveling to places where hepatitis is endemic.

DID YOU KNOW?

- Swimming in lakes and rivers may increase the chances of catching infections and diseases.

SANITATION IN RESTAURANTS

We often go to restaurants for lunches and dinners or snacks. It's easier for you to maintain hygiene in your kitchen because it's under your control, but ensuring a high standard of hygiene in restaurants is very difficult. If the food in restaurants is decomposed, it can lead to stomach infections, food poisoning, or worse.

WORDS TO UNDERSTAND

BRAND: a company's identity

DECOMPOSED: rotten

REGULATIONS: rules and laws

59

SANITATION IN RESTAURANTS

There are several reasons why sanitation and safe food-handling practices are important in restaurants. Sanitation helps maintain food quality. Even if customers don't fall sick, storing, preparing, or serving food in unsanitary conditions adversely affects the quality and taste. Sanitation also protects a restaurant's or company's brand. Keeping things clean and sanitary helps gain the trust of customers.

SANITATION LAWS

Sanitation is a legal requirement in all restaurants. Health inspectors inspect restaurants to make sure the local safety regulations are being followed. Sanitation helps prevent food poisoning outbreaks. Most food-related illnesses that are caused by restaurants are the result of unsanitary food-handling practices. Such incidents are not good for one's brand and can lead to a loss of brand value.

HOW TO KEEP RESTAURANTS HYGIENIC

Hygiene procedures are probably the most important safety and health concern of food service. Every restaurant faces the challenge of cleanliness and food safety. It is very important for its employees and managers to know and follow the rules of sanitation. Special care should be given to the washing and cleaning of utensils. It should be ensured that the cooks and waiters maintain a high degree of personal hygiene.

Check out this video to find out just how important restaurant health inspectors can be.

FOOD STORAGE

Some suggestions that can help with food storage are to never store food at room temperature. Bacteria can multiply at a rapid pace for the entire time that the food is kept at room temperature. Store food only in cool temperatures and always keep it covered. Storage areas, including refrigerators and freezers, should be clean and free of clutter. Adopt a "first in, first out" attitude toward food. When new food is delivered, the existing stock is placed in front so that it can be used first. Store different types of food separately in labeled containers. Food should be stored properly to prevent cross-contamination.

TRAVELING

You may need to select a restaurant while traveling. Be very careful of any slight change in the taste of food. Any sign of unhygienic material should immediately be brought to the attention of the restaurant manager.

DID YOU KNOW?

- In a recent survey, 65 percent of participants said that they chose restaurants based on food taste and freshness.

REGULAR CHECKUPS

There's an old saying, "An ounce of prevention is worth a pound of cure." But in our busy, fast-moving world, it's easy to forget the importance of prevention. We must remind ourselves that regular checkups are essential in maintaining good health. Taking proper care of your health from a young age can prevent many future health problems. It's important to find out if you suffer from a health problem before it is too late to cure it.

 WORDS TO UNDERSTAND

ABNORMALITIES: irregularities or defects

DIAGNOSIS: detection of an illness or health problem

IRRESPECTIVE: without regard to

62

WHY ARE CHECKUPS IMPORTANT?

Many people wonder why regular health checkups are necessary: why not just visit the doctor when a problem arises? It is important to remember that regular health checkups and tests can help find problems as soon as the first symptoms show. Early diagnosis of health conditions is advised because that is the time when your chances for treatment and cure are stronger.

AIM OF A CHECKUP

Getting the right health services, screenings, and treatments at the early stage of an illness can increase the chances of treating the illness and living a longer, healthier life. Hence, regular medical checkups are important, irrespective of your age, health, family history, or lifestyle choices.

MEDICAL HISTORY

As a part of your checkup, it is important to tell the doctor about your diet, exercise, medication (if you are taking any), family history of diseases—such as cancer, diabetes, asthma, or heart problems—or any symptoms you may be feeling. This information is vital, as it will keep your doctor well informed in case certain tests need to be recommended.

63

PHYSICAL EXAM

A health checkup begins with a physical examination. The doctor will check your height, weight, and blood pressure, including your heart rate. Your mouth, ears, skin, and abdomen may also be checked for any signs of abnormalities.

After your examination, the doctor should talk to you about any risk factors, and about habits you should change to maintain good health. The physician will also tell you any lab tests you need.

CHECKUP AND AGE

People of all ages need regular checkups. We should take the advice of our doctor seriously and go for all the lab tests he or she suggests. The extent of tests recommended is determined by any risk factors we may have based on our medical or family history.

DID YOU KNOW?

- The main goal of a checkup is to detect illness at an early stage, or better still, prevent its occurrence in the first place.

LAUNDRY HYGIENE

We all like to wear clean clothes every day. Appearance matters to all of us, and we all want to look clean and hygienic to make the right impression. Clothes are important reflections of our personality. But if they are not well cared-for, they can become unhygienic. It's very important to watch what we wear every day. It is important to ensure that your clothes are washed regularly.

WORDS TO UNDERSTAND

MINIMIZES: reduces

PRECAUTION: safeguards

REFLECTIONS: indicators of something

65

WHY IS LAUNDRY HYGIENE IMPORTANT?

Laundry hygiene is the practice that minimizes the spread of diseases on clothing and household linens. Items most likely to be affected with bacteria are those that come into direct contact with the body, e.g., underwear, personal towels, and facecloths. Laundry hygiene is essential for health. Even small precautions can save you from health troubles caused by dirty laundry.

LAUNDRY HYGIENE IN HOSPITALS

Laundry hygiene is not only important in households but also in places like hospitals and care homes. Laundry plays an essential role in patient comfort and in protecting the health of employees. It is important to note that laundry is a potential carrier of infections and hence special measures must be taken to ensure that the best hygiene levels are maintained. The laundry items themselves must not pose a threat to the patients' health. Dirty laundry can spread germs to other areas and needs to be handled carefully.

HOW TO KEEP LAUNDRY HYGIENIC

Apart from regular clothes, pillow covers, curtains, bedsheets, quilts, towels, and tablecloths must also be washed and changed regularly to give them a fresh look and keep them germ-free.

IMPORTANT POINTS TO REMEMBER

We shouldn't store dirty laundry for long periods and bring it into contact with clean laundry. It's important to store your dirty laundry in a separate area so that it can't spread germs to other areas.

DID YOU KNOW?

- Dangerous organisms are present in home laundry, and 44 percent of washing machines contain bacteria.

67

PUBLIC HEALTH AND HYGIENE

Public health can be understood as the organized efforts of society and individuals to ensure the prevention of diseases and to promote health. It deals with the promotion of a healthy lifestyle, as well as improving the health of communities. It involves intensive research into unhygienic practices, diseases, causes of their spread, and how to prevent them. It includes epidemiology, environmental health, and health education.

WORDS TO UNDERSTAND

EPIDEMIOLOGY: the study of how diseases spread and what can be done to control them

PROMOTION: encouragement

SURROUNDINGS: environments or settings

EPIDEMIOLOGY

Epidemiology is the investigation and study of diseases, causes of their spread, and methods of prevention. It is one of the branches of public health. Epidemiologists study the lifestyle of people in a community and changes in population. They do extensive research to find out the root cause of diseases and how dangerous they can be. Epidemiologists research solutions to deal with the health issues of communities.

HEALTH EDUCATION

The goal of health education is to spread health and hygiene awareness. Implementing health and hygiene programs in schools and communities to teach people how to prevent injuries and the spread of diseases is the main objective of health education. It encourages people to make healthy choices.

PUBLIC HEALTH PROFESSIONALS

Public health professionals are people who take the required actions and measures to keep people healthy. They monitor the health of the people of a community, detecting and investigating health problems. They carry out research to discover

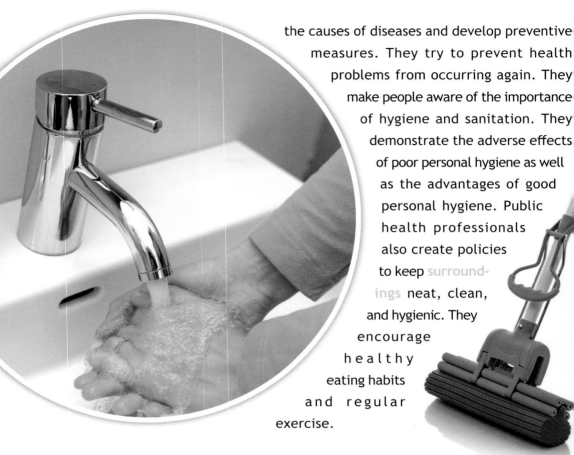

the causes of diseases and develop preventive measures. They try to prevent health problems from occurring again. They make people aware of the importance of hygiene and sanitation. They demonstrate the adverse effects of poor personal hygiene as well as the advantages of good personal hygiene. Public health professionals also create policies to keep surroundings neat, clean, and hygienic. They encourage healthy eating habits and regular exercise.

PUBLIC HEALTH PRESERVATION

Public health can be preserved in several ways, such as eating a healthy and nutritious diet, and following good hygiene practices at home, in schools, hospitals, and other social centers, as well as on the streets. Environmental health and hygiene is also an integral part of public health, as our surroundings influence our health.

DID YOU KNOW?

- In 1854, John Snow identified a public water pump situated in London's Soho district to be the cause of the outbreak of cholera.

TEXT-DEPENDENT QUESTIONS

1. What is hygiene?

2. Why is food hygiene important?

3. What are some tips to keep water supplies safe?

4. What are some hygiene measures taken by schools?

5. What is occupational hygiene?

6. What are some aspects of environmental hygiene?

7. What are the effects of poor waste management?

8. Why is sterilization important?

9. What's usually the dirtiest part of a home?

10. What's the single most important thing you can do to practice good hygiene?

RESEARCH PROJECTS

1. Find out more about the history of hygiene. What were some past attitudes on bathing, and how did they change over time? What historical events contributed to that evolution?

2. Assess the hygiene of your home. Consider the kitchen, bedrooms, bathrooms, and so on. What problems do you notice? Lead a discussion with your family about what you all can do to make your home more hygienic.

3. Ask your school nurse if you can interview him or her about hygiene at school. What problems does the nurse encounter? What could be done to make your school more hygienic?

4. Using this book and other sources in the Further Reading section, create a pamphlet or comic book that advises people your age about how to improve their hygiene.

amino acid: an organic molecule that is the building block of proteins.

antibody: a protein in the blood that fights off substances the body thinks are dangerous.

antioxidant: a substance that fights against free radicals, molecules in the body that can damage other cells.

biofortification: the process of improving the nutritional value of crops through breeding or genetic modification.

calories: units of heat used to indicate the amount of energy that foods will produce in the human body.

carbohydrates: substances found in certain foods (such as bread, rice, and potatoes) that provide the body with heat and energy and are made of carbon, hydrogen, and oxygen.

carcinogen: something that causes cancer.

cardiovascular: of or relating to the heart and blood vessels.

carnivorous: meat-eating.

cholesterol: a soft, waxy substance present in all parts of the body, including the skin, muscles, liver, and intestines.

collagen: a fibrous protein that makes up much of the body's connective tissues.

deficiency: a lack of something, such as a nutrient in one's diet.

derivative: a product that is made from another source; for example, malt comes from barley, making it a barley derivative.

diabetes: a disease in which the body's ability to produce the hormone insulin is impaired.

dietary supplements: products taken orally that contain one or more ingredient (such as vitamins or amino acids) that are intended to supplement one's diet and are not considered food.

electrolytes: substances (such as sodium or calcium) that are ions in the body regulating the flow of nutrients into and waste products out of cells.

enzyme: a protein that starts or accelerates an action or process within the body.

flexible: applies to something that can be readily bent, twisted, or folded without any sign of injury.

food additive: a product added to a food to improve flavor, appearance, nutritional value, or shelf life.

genetically modified organism (GMO): a plant or animal that has had its genetic material altered to create new characteristics.

growth hormone: a substance either naturally produced by the body or synthetically made that stimulates growth in animals or plants.

herbicide: a substance designed to kill unwanted plants, such as weeds.

hydration: to supply with ample fluid or moisture.

macronutrients: nutrients required in large amounts for the health of living organisms, including proteins, fats, and carbohydrates.

metabolism: the chemical process by which living cells produce energy.

micronutrients: nutrients required in very small amounts for the health of living organisms.

nutritional profile: the nutritional makeup of given foods, including the balance of vitamins, minerals, proteins, fats, and other components.

obesity: a condition in which excess body fat has amassed to the point where it causes ill-health effects.

pasteurization: a process that kills microorganisms, making certain foods and drinks safer to consume.

pesticide: a substance designed to kill insects or other organisms that can cause damage to plants or animals.

processed food: food that has been refined before resale, often with additional fats, sugars, sodium, and other additives.

protein: a nutrient found in food (as in meat, milk, eggs, and beans) that is made up of many amino acids joined together, is a necessary part of the diet, and is essential for normal cell structure and function.

protein complementation: the dietary practice of combining different plant-based foods to get all of the essential amino acids.

refined: when referring to grains or flours, describing those that have been processed to remove elements of the whole grain.

sustainable: a practice that can be successfully maintained over a long period of time.

vegan: a person who does not eat meat, poultry, fish, dairy, or other products sourced from animals.

vegetarian: a person who does not eat meat, poultry, or fish.

whole grain: grains that have been minimally processed and contain all three main parts of the grain—the bran, the germ, and the endosperm.

workout: a practice or exercise to test or improve one's fitness for athletic competition, ability, or performance.

FURTHER READING

FOOD AND AGRICULTURAL ORGANIZATION. *Food Handler's Handbook*. Washington, DC: 2017.

SHAW, IAN. *Food Safety: The Science of Keeping Food Safe*. Hoboken, NJ: John Wiley & Sons, 2018.

SIMONS, RAE. *Healthy Skin*. Broomall, PA: Mason Crest, 2014.

SMITH, SARAH. *Etiquette for Success: School*. Broomall, PA: Mason Crest, 2019.

INTERNET RESOURCES

FOODSAFETY.GOV

This site, run by the U.S. Department of Health and Human Services, is a gateway to anything you need to know about food safety topics.
https://www.foodsafety.gov/

PERSONAL HYGIENE FOR TEENS AND TWEENS

The Johnson & Johnson company hosts a thorough resource for all sorts of hygiene questions.
https://www.healthyessentials.com/baby-child-solutions/personal-hygiene-for-teens-tweens

TEEN HYGIENE TIPS

This detailed article from WebMD provides lots of advice for teens.
https://www.webmd.com/parenting/features/teen-hygiene#1

WELLNESS

Teen Vogue collects its articles about all aspects of wellness, from fitness and diet to self-care and mental health.
https://www.teenvogue.com/wellness/

INDEX

Photo Credits

Photographs sourced by Macaw Media, except for the following:
Cover and p. 1: © photopixel | Shutterstock, © Oleg GawriloFF | Shutterstock, © IMAGE LAGOON | Shutterstock, © belka_35 | Shutterstock, © Lipskiy | Shutterstock, © p_ponomareva | Shutterstock; p. 2: © Kongsky | Dreamstime, © Jamakosy | Dreamstime; p. 3: © New Africa | Shutterstock; p. 5: © photopixel | Shutterstock; p. 6: © Jasmina | Dreamstime; p. 7: © Sucharn | Dreamstime; p. 9: © Bignai | Dreamstime; p. 10: © Dimarik16 | Dreamstime, © Nadya Nadal | Shutterstock; p. 11: © Wave Break Media Ltd | Dreamstime; p. 13: © Hyrman | Dreamstime; p. 14: © Ggw1962 | Dreamstime; p. 16: © Ben Schonewille | Dreamstime; p. 19: © Luis Louro | Dreamstime; p. 23: © Kiryl Balbatunou | Dreamstime; p. 25: © Gustavo Toledo | Dreamstime; p. 27: © Oksana Krasyuk | Dreamstime, © Marko Volkmar | Dreamstime; p. 29: © Jevtic | Dreamstime; p. 30: © Mackon | Dreamstime; p. 31: © IMAGE LAGOON | Shutterstock; p. 34: © Natallia Yaumenenka | Dreamstime; p. 35: © Jamakosy | Dreamstime, © Olena Yakobchuk | Dreamstime; p. 36: © Lisa F. Young | Dreamstime; p. 37: © Mocker | Dreamstime; p. 39: © Chernetskaya | Dreamstime; p. 40: © Darren Brode | Dreamstime; p. 41: © Valerii Honcharuk | Dreamstime; p. 42: © Pic.r | Dreamstime, © David Franklin | Dreamstime; p. 44: © Stuart Miles | Dreamstime; p. 45: © Igor Mojzes | Dreamstime; p. 47: © Steven Day | Dreamstime; p. 48: © Alexandr Kornienko | Dreamstime; p. 49: © Luckynick | Dreamstime, © Artmim | Dreamstime; p. 50: © Anton Maltsev | Dreamstime; p. 51: © Sabphoto | Dreamstime; p. 52: © Anna Anisimova | Dreamstime; p. 53: © Toxitz | Dreamstime, © Madhourse | Dreamstime; p. 54: © Vchalup | Dreamstime, © Dimarik16 | Dreamstime; p. 55: © Sittipong Leetangwattana | Dreamstime; p. 56: © Mimagephotography | Dreamstime; p. 57: © Alena Brozova | Dreamstime; p. 58: © Konstantin Nechaev | Dreamstime; p. 59: © Auremar | Dreamstime, © Max Lashcheuski | Dreamstime; p. 60: © Zorandim | Dreamstime; p. 61: © Andrii Hrytsenko | Dreamstime; p. 62: © Settaphan Rummanee | Dreamstime, © Kuprevich | Dreamstime; p. 63: © Gabriel Blaj | Dreamstime; p. 64: © Alexander Raths | Dreamstime, p. 65: © Yana Bardichevska | Dreamstime; p. 66: © Auremar | Dreamstime, © Chernetskaya | Dreamstime; p. 67: © Vladakela | Dreamstime, © Martinmark | Dreamstime; p. 68: © Motortion | Dreamstime; p. 69: © Auremar | Dreamstime; p. 70: © Sabina Pensek | Dreamstime, © Valio84sl | Dreamstime; p. 71: © Neurobite | Dreamstime, © Mihalec | Dreamstime; p. 72: © Jiri Bursik | Dreamstime; p. 73: © Sergey Kolesnikov | Dreamstime; p. 75: © Karina Bakalyan | Dreamstime; p. 76: © Liljam | Dreamstime